NO PETS ALLOWED

D1176809

Published simultaneously in Canada and the UK in 2010.
Distribution and representation in the UK by Turnaround.
www.turnaround-uk.com
Released in the US in 2011

Text copyright © 2010 by Irene N. Watts
Illustrations copyright © 2010 by Kathryn E. Shoemaker

All rights reserved. No part of this publication may be reproduced, stored
in a retrieval system or transmitted, in any form or by any means, without
prior written permission of the publisher or, in the case of photocopying
or other reprographic copying, a licence from Access Copyright.
The right of Irene N. Watts to be identified as the author and for
Kathryn E. Shoemaker to be identified as the illustrator of this work
has been asserted by them in accordance with the Copyright, Design
and Patents Act, 1988.

LIBRARY AND ARCHIVES CANADA CATALOGUING IN PUBLICATION
Watts, Irene N., 1931-
    No pets allowed / Irene Watts ; illustrated by Kathryn Shoemaker.

ISBN 978-1-896580-94-4

    I. Shoemaker, Kathryn E II. Title.

PS8595.A873N67 2010   jC813'.54   C2010-902920-8

CATALOGUING-IN-PUBLICATION DATA AVAILABLE FROM THE BRITISH LIBRARY.

Book & cover design by Elisa Gutiérrez.
Title and chapter numbers drawn by hand by Kathryn E. Shoemaker.

Inside pages printed on FSC certified paper using vegetable-based inks.

Manufactured by Sunrise Printing
Manufactured in Chilliwack, BC, Canada in October 2010
10 9 8 7 6 5 4 3 2 1

The publisher acknowledges the support of the Canada Council for the
Arts. The publisher also wishes to thank the Government of British
Columbia for the financial support it has extended through
the book publishing tax credit program and the British Columbia
Arts Council. The publisher also acknowledges the financial support
of the Government of Canada through the Canada Book Fund and
Livres Canada Books for our publishing activities.

Canada Council   Conseil des Arts
for the Arts   du Canada

BRITISH
COLUMBIA
ARTS COUNCIL

Irene N. Watts

NO
PETS
ALLOWED

illustrations by
Kathryn E. Shoemaker

VANCOUVER • LONDON

For William and Zoltan—I.N.W.

To my sweet Will—K.E.S.

CONTENTS

CHAPTER ONE

No Pets

O n Friday afternoon Matthew Wade ran out of the schoolyard, waited for the crossing guard to wave him across the street and reached his building in four and a quarter minutes. Matthew always ran faster when he felt happy. Well, he didn't exactly feel happy, but he felt much better than he had on Monday, which was his first day at Baldwin Elementary School.

How could he be happy without Lucky? Matthew's grandfather had brought Lucky home a year earlier on his seventh birthday and said, "This little runt needs looking after. Think you can feed him regularly, clean up after him, take him for walks and teach him not to chase the chickens? Puppies are lots of work. You'll have to train him to be a good watchdog!"

The tips of Matthew's ears turned red; the smile on his face almost split it in two. He tried to hug

both the pup and his grandfather, but his arms weren't quite long enough.

"I'll do everything right, you'll see. Thanks, Grandpa, this is the greatest birthday present ever. I'll call the pup Lucky, because this is my lucky day."

Lucky left puddles in all the wrong places and Matthew cleaned them up. Lucky howled for his mother in the night, he howled at the dark and he didn't like thunderstorms, but Matthew got up to comfort him.

Lucky learned fast. He and Matthew were inseparable. Wherever Matthew went, Lucky came too. Not anymore. Now that he had moved to Vancouver, he and Lucky were hundreds of miles apart.

Matthew was out of breath by the time he reached his apartment building. He stared at the sign on the door: NO PETS ALLOWED.

Every day Matthew hoped for a miracle—that one day he'd look up and the sign would be gone. But every day the letters stared back at him: NO PETS ALLOWED. Matthew felt like getting a ladder, climbing up and taking the sign down.

I'd like to go and dig a deep hole and bury that old sign somewhere, so no one will ever find it.

Why did they have to move to Vancouver? Mum said the move would be a great opportunity, a challenge for both of them. Best of all her new job had great hours so she and Matthew could be home at the same time. And Vancouver was so near the ocean and had so many trees! But it didn't feel so wonderful to Matthew. How could he enjoy anything without Lucky?

This was Matthew's first visit to a city as big as Vancouver. What was so wonderful about it? He didn't think much of it: noisy traffic day and night, too many people rushing off somewhere. Worst of all, there was no Lucky to come home to.

Matthew sprinted down the hallway of his building.

He was stopped by a stern voice. "Wipe your feet when you come in," said the manager of the building.

"Sorry, I forgot!"

The manager glared at him. He wore a checkered shirt with the sleeves rolled up, showing strong muscled arms. His jeans were tucked inside his work boots, and a cellphone was clipped to his belt.

"You're the new kid from apartment 103, aren't you? My name's Leo, *Mister* Leo. I've been resident manager of this building for ten years. I make sure the rules are kept. You'd better remember that. Wipe your feet when you come in. Don't run in the hallways. No noise after ten o'clock at night and absolutely NO PETS ALLOWED. Is that clear?" He stared at Matthew until Matthew went back and wiped his feet on the front doormat.

"Right, don't forget again."

Matthew didn't answer, but for a moment he was almost glad that Lucky was back on the farm! Mister Leo sounded as though he didn't like anyone, not kids or dogs or even grown-ups.

CHAPTER TWO

"You promised"

"**M**um, you're home early. Great, I'm starved." Matthew threw down his backpack.

"How was school today?"

Mrs. Wade put two oatmeal cookies on a plate, poured Matthew some apple juice and went on unpacking the groceries.

"Okay, I guess. Mum, when can we go and visit Lucky?"

"We've only just got here," his mother said. "You have to be patient. We'll save up and visit at Christmas." Mrs. Wade brushed Matthew's hair out of his eyes. He pulled away from her and took the spare dog leash he always carried with him out of his backpack.

"That's too long to wait. Lucky will miss us. He doesn't know why I'm not there to play with him

or to take him for walks. He's waiting for me. He's lonely."

"Grandpa will take good care of Lucky," she reassured him.

"Lucky hates sleeping by himself. He's still afraid of the dark and of thunderstorms." Matthew's foot beat a tattoo against the table leg.

"Stop exaggerating, Matthew. Lucky's a farm dog, almost full grown. He hasn't been afraid since he was a puppy, and you know it. He's fine."

Matthew's mother smiled at him.

"I'm not fine." Matthew swung the leash back and forth, and his mother grabbed it before it hit the chair.

"When are we going to find a place that allows dogs? You promised," Matthew said.

"Sit down and listen. Look at me. I said I'd *try* to find a place where we can keep a dog. And I *have* tried. You know that. There aren't many apartments for rent that take dogs. We have to live close enough to school so that you can walk there by yourself. We need to live close to transit so that I can get to work without a car. The West End has all that, and for now this is the best I can do."

Matthew could tell his mother was losing her patience. "I guess so, but I'm lonely without Lucky. It's lonely living in the city and being new in school."

"I miss Lucky too. We won't always be new. We'll get to like it here," Matthew's mother said.

"I won't! Nothing's the same as it used to be. I hate it here!" Matthew frowned at his mother.

"You're hungry. You'll feel better after supper. Don't say you won't. We're having pineapple and ham pizza."

Mrs. Wade went into the kitchen and Matthew got into his favourite thinking position, one that almost always worked for him: he stood on his head, feet hardly touching the wall, and counted

to one hundred, his best score ever. Collapsing on the floor, he practiced an imitation of Lucky when he was happy. "*Woof woof.*"

Mrs. Wade called out, "Not so loud. Mister Leo will think we have a dog. We don't need that kind of trouble. Wash your hands for supper. And then, why don't you write a letter to Grandpa and he can read it to Lucky."

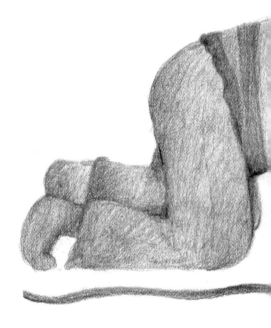

CHAPTER THREE

An Invisible dog

Matthew's bedroom window overlooked the parking lot. He watched Mister Leo vacuuming the inside of his red pickup truck.

I bet it doesn't even need cleaning, Matthew thought.

He swung his leash like a lasso and pulled it back before it hit the glass. Then he draped the leash around the back of his neck. The leather felt good against his bare skin.

If only Lucky were here. If only I had a dog that belonged to me, the city wouldn't be so bad. How can I grow up to be a dog trainer without a dog? What am I supposed to do, train an imaginary dog?

Matthew undressed, dropped his clothes on the floor, shrugged his T-shirt over his head and threw himself onto the bed. He stared up at a damp patch on the ceiling. When he was little, his

mum had stuck stars all over his bedroom ceiling. He used to like the way they glittered against the blue background.

I'm getting too old for stars. In ten years' time, I'll be eighteen. I'll have trained hundreds of dogs by then, he thought.

He turned over onto his side so that he could look out the window. It was neat watching the way the setting sun reflected off the other buildings. For a little while each evening it looked as if the city was on fire.

If there were a fire, Lucky wouldn't even know about it. He'd be too far away to bark us awake.

Matthew imagined Lucky lying beside him.

What did you do today while I was in school? Did you chase after gophers? I wish we were running the way we used to. I wish we could keep on running through the grass forever.

Just then Matthew heard a noise outside. He sat up and listened. Then he ran to the window, opened it and looked out. Mister Leo had finished cleaning his red truck. The lot was quiet. Then there was that noise again. This time it sounded like it was coming from under the bed.

Maybe it's a kitten or a rat or a mouse? No way! How would anything on four legs get in without Mister Leo knowing about it? Suppose something had. Would his mum let him keep it? A mouse would make a good pet. Mice are no trouble. They squeak really quietly.

Matthew slid off the bed and lay on his stomach on the floor. He reached under the bed and found the slipper he'd lost the day before. Something furry brushed against his fingers.

Then his mother came in.

"Have you lost something? Oh good, you've found your slipper. Hop into bed."

She picked up Matthew's jeans, folded them and hung them on the back of his chair.

"I wish you'd remember to do that. Now, where did we get to?" Mrs. Wade sat down and opened *Tom's Midnight Garden.*

"The part where Tom gets up in the night and hears the hall clock strike thirteen times, and Tom goes through the back door and sees the garden."

After his mother had finished reading the chapter, Matthew said, "Just before you came in to read to me, I heard a weird noise under the bed."

His mother knelt down and looked.

"Nothing there, not even a spider. Sleep well." She kissed the top of Matthew's head, shut the window and went out.

It sounded almost the way Lucky did when he first came to the farm and didn't know how to bark properly.

Matthew made a sound like that in the back of his throat, remembering Lucky's half growl, half whimper. He felt for the flashlight he kept

under his pillow and jumped out of bed to take another look. Mum was right, there was nothing there.

He climbed back into bed and closed his eyes. He was almost asleep when he felt something cold and wet lick his cheek.

"Stop it, Lucky," he said without opening his eyes. "Lucky?" He sat up, fully awake now. "It can't be. I must've been dreaming."

But something, or someone, was pulling at the corner of his blanket. Slowly the blanket began to slide off his bed. Matthew grabbed it. He looked down and saw a rough tongue licking his fingers. It wasn't Lucky. Instead, a brown and oatmeal-coloured puppy was doing his best to reach him.

Matthew stroked the shaggy ears and soft fur under the puppy's chin. "You're just a pup, aren't you? Are you real? Were you there a minute ago when Mum looked under the bed? You remind me of Fred, back home in my grade two class. You know what? Your hair falls over your eyes just like his did. He was the fastest runner in the class. I only ever beat him once. I bet you can run too. I'll call you Fred, and we'll go running together. And I'll teach you how to bark properly, the way I taught Lucky. "*Woof woof!*"

Mrs. Wade hurried in. "It's after ten o'clock. No more barking! Go to sleep." She tucked the quilt

firmly under Matthew's chin. "Good night," she said, and left the room.

Matthew whispered, "This place doesn't allow pets, Fred, but Mum didn't see you, so Mister Leo won't either."

"Tomorrow I'll start your training." He snuggled Fred under the quilt and went to sleep.

CHAPTER FOUR

"No Sneaking around"

After breakfast on Saturday, there were chores to be done.

"Finish cleaning up your room so we can go for a walk, it's going to be a beautiful day," Mrs. Wade said.

"Great, Fred needs a run and I have to start training him!" said Matthew.

Mrs. Wade looked puzzled. "Who's Fred?" she asked.

"Fred's my new dog. He's invisible and only I can see him. Here, boy, come on, don't be scared. Say hello to my mum." Matthew held out his hand to Fred, who was cowering under the table.

"Matthew, since when have you had an imaginary dog? You never mentioned him before."

"I haven't? I guess not. I found him last night after you finished reading to me. That was the noise I heard under the bed. I drew a picture of

him before breakfast, to put in my report. I'll go get it. Stay, boy. Good dog." Matthew ran into his bedroom and came back with his exercise book.

"See the way I've drawn his eyes and the way he holds his head? What do you think?"

"I like it a lot," said Matthew's mother. "When I was a little girl, a bit younger than you are now, I wanted a pet. I was desperate to have a kitten, but my mother said I had to wait till I was older. I thought of nothing else. Finally I pretended to be one. When my mum asked me something, I'd purr and she'd tell me not to be rude."

"Did you ever get your pet?"

"Yes, for my seventh birthday. My dad said he was tired of having a daughter who didn't know whether she was a girl or a kitten."

"That sounds like Grandpa," Matthew said. "Do you think that's why he brought Lucky home for me, because he didn't want me pretending I was a dog? Woof! Woof!"

"Why don't you write about Lucky in your report too?" his mother said.

"I'm going to write about both Lucky and Fred. Come on, Fred, help me clean up my room so we can go out."

They walked partway along the seawall. Then Mrs. Wade sat down on a log and watched Matthew throw sticks for Fred, and laughed at him trying to teach Fred to fetch.

When they got home, it was time for lunch. Mrs. Wade said Matthew could play outside for ten more minutes while she made them peanut butter and banana sandwiches.

The small plot of grass outside the front doors of the building was trimmed short. Not a blade of grass was out of place.

"I bet Mister Leo comes out at night and cuts off any stalk that dares to grow taller than the others," Matthew told Fred, giggling.

They wrestled, rolling over and over on the patch of lawn, barking and laughing.

"What do you think you're playing at, you young hooligan?" an angry voice yelled. "Get off the grass before you ruin my lawn!"

Matthew stood up quickly, stumbling over the leash, which had wrapped itself around his ankles. All he wanted was to get away from Mister Leo's mean stare.

"What are you doing with that leash?" Mister Leo pointed to the sign. "Can't you read? NO PETS ALLOWED! I won't have you smuggling a dog into my building, or any other kind of pet. No sneaking around, you hear me?"

"I wasn't doing any harm. I was only playing," Matthew said. He wasn't used to being called names. He picked up Fred and the leash and ran inside, remembering to wipe his feet. He could feel Mister Leo's eyes on his back.

"Stop panting, Fred, he'll hear you. Pets aren't allowed here." Matthew peeked over his shoulder

and saw that the manager was still standing there, watching him.

The elderly couple who lived in 102 said, "Hello," and Colonel Banks, who reminded him of Grandpa, said, "Brought your dog's leash, I see. You must miss him, coming from the prairies."

Matthew said, "Hello," and, "Yes, sir, I do," and went inside his own apartment, thinking not everyone in the building was as mean as Mister Leo.

CHAPTER FIVE

Monika

By Thursday afternoon all the students had read their reports on pets, except for one girl and Matthew.

Reading aloud, by alphabetical order, means it's a long wait if your last name starts with a W.

By the time Julia got to the part about cleaning out her hamster cage, Matthew's mind had wandered off into his favourite daydream, the one where he gets home from school and his mother tells him the great news: "Guess what? I've found a place close by that allows pets!" Then they rush off to the bus depot, buy their tickets and bring Lucky home where he belongs.

Matthew breathed a long happy sigh. He had just reached the bit in his daydream where Fred and Lucky meet for the first time, when he heard his name called. He looked up and saw all the kids staring at him.

Monika, who sat in front of him, turned around, peered at him short-sightedly and hissed, "Mrs. Hart called your name twice!"

Matthew stood up, his face red, and mumbled, "Sorry." He walked to the front of the class and began to read.

My Pets, by Matthew Wade

I have two dogs. The first one is called Lucky. I've had him since he was six weeks old. When we moved here from Alberta, we had to leave him behind on my grandfather's farm. Lucky is a cross-country Labrador. That's a big dog, so he needs to run. As soon as we've settled down, we'll bring him to Vancouver to live with us.

My other dog is called Fred. I just got him a couple of days ago. He's a brown and oatmeal-coloured terrier puppy. He doesn't know he's a small dog yet. He thinks he's a watchdog, and barks to warn me if there are strangers around. He doesn't like wearing his leash, but he has to, because of the traffic.

When we go out, he gets excited and runs and stumbles over my feet. His training is going well. He understands what "stay" and "sit" and "fetch" mean. I hope to be a dog trainer when I grow up."

Everyone applauded when Matthew held up his drawing of Fred.

Mrs. Hart smiled at him and said, "Very nice work, Matthew," and then the buzzer went for the end of school.

Monika hung around. Matthew could tell she wanted to talk to him.

"It's my turn to read tomorrow," Monika said. "My report's on fish. Three of my fish died last week. I hate it when my dad calls me for breakfast in the morning. He always shouts, 'Monika, honey, hurry or you'll be late for school. Another one of your fish died.' Then I can't eat and he gets mad at me."

"It's not your fault that fish don't live as long as dogs," Matthew said. "There's not much you can do with fish, is there? I mean, you can't take them for walks."

He tried not to laugh at the thought of taking goldfish out for a run.

Monika noticed.

"You can so do a lot with fish! I train them to swim toward me before I throw in the fish food. My new goldfish makes faces at me. He knows me."

"I hope he lives a long time," Matthew said, feeling sorry for her. "Fish are good pets to have. They're quiet, so no one can tell you they're making too much noise. See you tomorrow."

Matthew put on his backpack and headed out of the classroom. Monika caught up with him outside.

"Is your dog waiting for you at the gate? I can't see him anywhere."

"That's because he's waiting for me at home." Matthew wished Monika would stop asking questions. He didn't want to talk about Fred.

"When can I see him? Can I come over to your place sometime?"

Matthew didn't know what to say. *How am I going to explain that I'm the only person in the world who can see Fred?*

"Sometime, I guess. I'd better go home now. My mum will be back from work," he said.

"My dad says there aren't many places around here that allow dogs. That's why I keep fish—dogs aren't allowed where I live."

Monika chewed a strand of her hair, adding, "Are you sure you didn't make up all those dogs you read about in class?"

Matthew glared at her.

"'*All those dogs?*' I never said '*all*'; I said two. TWO! Are you calling me a liar?"

He opened his backpack, pulled out Lucky's old leash and held it up to show Monika.

"This is Fred's leash, and I'm going home now to play with him. Why don't you go and feed your dumb fish and leave me alone?"

Monika said, "I don't know why you're so mad. I was only asking."

Then she ran out of the schoolyard and waited for the crossing guard to stop the cars for her.

Matthew was glad Monica went home in the opposite direction from him. He hurried away.

Fred was waiting behind the front door of the apartment. He jumped up, trying to lick Matthew's face. Matthew bent down and ruffled his ears.

"It's not many dogs that get to be invisible. You're a special dog, Fred, a million times better than a fish, even if I'm the only one who can see you," he said.

CHAPTER SIX

A Visit from Mister Leo

"**M**um, I'm home. I'm starved!" Matthew ran into the kitchen where his mother was unloading groceries. Mrs. Wade poured her son a glass of chocolate milk and set out cheese and crackers for his snack.

"How did your report go?"

"Okay, I guess," Matthew said. "Here, boy." He held out a piece of cheese for Fred. His mother told him to stop playing with his food.

There was a knock at the door.

"It's the manager, Mister Leo."

Mrs. Wade went to let him in.

"Stay, boy." Matthew put his hand on Fred's head.

"I'm afraid it's not very tidy, Mister Leo," said Mrs. Wade. "I've just come in from work."

"No problem, Mrs. Wade. There are a couple of things we need to discuss."

"And how can we help you?" Mrs. Wade said politely, putting the last of the tins away and folding the bags for recycling.

"Is your kid keeping a dog? Every time I see him, I hear barking and he looks kind of guilty, like he's hiding something…"

Matthew kept his hand on Fred's collar, waiting, listening.

"My son's name is Matthew, Mister Leo," Mrs. Wade said, interrupting the manager.

Mister Leo turned to Matthew. "I'll come straight to the point. Matthew, are you hiding a pet anywhere on the premises?"

"Have you or anyone else ever *seen* my son with a dog? The only dog we own is this one." Mrs. Wade took the photograph in its gold frame down from the centre of the mantelpiece and showed it to Mister Leo. "Here is our dog, Lucky, with Matthew and his grandfather. Lucky lives hundreds of miles away in Alberta."

Mister Leo stepped over to the table, cleared his throat and, looking right at Matthew and Fred, said, "It's come to my attention that you carry a dog leash around with you. Now I'd call that pretty suspicious. Maybe you can explain why you carry a leash if you don't keep a dog. I want a straight answer, kid. Are you hiding any kind of pet—dog, cat, mouse, snake, pig, iguana?"

Matthew spluttered into his glass of milk. *Iguana?*

"Don't slurp!" Matthew's mother said. She turned to Mister Leo.

"I'm surprised that you won't accept my word, Mister Leo, and that you continue to make your accusations. Do you see or hear any sign of a pet? I think you owe us an apology."

Matthew could tell that his mum was getting mad.

"I'm not accusing anyone *yet*. Matthew, weren't you playing with an animal on the front lawn yesterday?"

"Well, I *was* playing with Fred," Matthew said.

Mister Leo nodded, a satisfied grin on his face.

"I thought so. No smoke without fire, no bark without a dog. Glad someone's telling the truth around here. Fred will have to go, and right now. No exceptions!"

"Mister Leo, please listen a moment. I don't think you quite understand the situation. The thing about Fred is that..."

"Mum, don't!" Matthew tried to interrupt to stop his mum from telling Mister Leo any more.

"Matthew, be quiet! You see, Mister Leo, my son misses Lucky very much and Fred is a..."

Mister Leo wouldn't let her finish what she was trying to say. "I don't make the rules, Mrs. Wade. I enforce them, and if tenants don't like it, well you know what happens next!"

"I know, we'll be evicted, but it's not what you think. Fred is an imaginary dog!"

Mister Leo stared at Matthew and his mother in disbelief. "Now I've heard everything! Nice try, Mrs. Wade, but it won't work. Either this...this *Fred* goes, or you do!"

"Please listen! Fred's a pretend dog."

Pretend? Matthew's face went beet red and he said, "He's not pretend. Fred's real! I'm training him and no one's going to take him away from me."

He stormed into his bedroom and slammed the door.

"Mister Leo, I give you my word. There is no pet here. Matthew is lonely—he's had to adjust to a lot of new things. Fred really is only pretend. I guess it's the only way my son can deal with losing his real dog. I'm sorry he behaved badly. I know you're just doing your job."

"Right, we'll leave it like that for now." Mister Leo didn't sound convinced. "I'll let myself out."

After Mister Leo left the apartment, Matthew stuck his head round the door.

"Has he gone? Don't be mad at me Mum."

"Come here!"

Mrs. Wade gave Matthew a hug. "I *am* mad. You were very rude. But I'm mad at the rules too and mad at myself. I wish we could find a place we can afford that will take Lucky. For now this is the best I can do."

"Okay. Fred's waiting for me to play with him. I'll remind him not to bark!"

CHAPTER SEVEN

Fire

That night Matthew found it hard to fall asleep. He was still upset. If only there was something he could do to change the rules about keeping a pet. Over and over in his head, he heard the mean way Mister Leo had said, "No smoke without fire," and the way the manager had glared at him.

"Like I was a thief or something, you heard him, didn't you, Fred?" Matthew whispered. "It would serve him right if I *was* hiding Lucky under my bed."

At last he fell asleep, holding the leash.

Suddenly he woke up. Fred was trying to attract his attention, pulling the leash out of his hand. "What's the matter, boy? It's the middle of the night. Look how dark it is outside. We can't go for a run now. Settle down, okay?"

After a few minutes, Matthew struggled awake again. "What's that weird smell?"

Matthew began to cough and splutter, choking. "I can smell burning. Maybe there's a fire. Is that why you woke me? Good dog. There's smoke coming in under the door. We've got to warn Mum!"

Matthew grabbed his sweater, held it over his mouth and crawled toward the bedroom door.

"Mum, wake up quick! There's a fire! Call 9-1-1, Mum!" Matthew couldn't breathe. He picked up Fred with his free hand, trying to cover both their mouths with his sweater, and held him close to his chest. Mrs. Wade ran toward her son.

"Matthew, it's all right, you're having a bad dream. I'm here. Open your eyes. We're all quite safe."

Mrs. Wade led Matthew toward a chair, and made him sit down. Then she knelt down in front of him. "Open your eyes. There is no fire. The smoke alarm isn't ringing. I'll open the front door and check everything."

Mrs. Wade unlocked the door. There wasn't a sound; no alarm bell rang.

"There isn't even a wisp of smoke anywhere," Mrs. Wade said, but Matthew wasn't listening to her.

"Mum, Fred woke me. He's a hero. He smelled the smoke. We've got to get out of here. We can climb out of the window. It's not far to the ground." Matthew ran to the window and tried to open it.

Mrs. Wade grabbed Matthew and led him to the front door and showed him the corridor. Everything

looked the same as always. There was no fire; not even a hint of smoke.

They went back inside, and Matthew's mother made him sit down again. She brought him a glass of water, doing her best to reassure him.

"You had a nightmare, and now it's all over. Look, the corridor is empty. Our smoke alarms were all tested the day we moved in, don't you remember?"

"I guess I must have been dreaming, but it was so real, Mum. I was coughing and choking. I could hardly breathe." Matthew wiped his face.

"I'll make us some hot chocolate," his mother said.

Just before Matthew went back to sleep he said, "If it was only a bad dream, why did Fred smell the smoke too? Why did he wake me up? How come we had the same nightmare?"

"Go to sleep, and stop worrying. You imagine Fred, so he dreams the same things you do."

Mrs. Wade went out on tiptoe, leaving the bedroom door ajar.

She didn't hear Matthew murmur before he fell asleep, "Thanks for waking me up, Fred."

CHAPTER EIGHT

An Invitation

At recess next morning, Monika hung down beside Matthew on the monkey bars.

"I put an invitation on your desk. It's for my birthday party on Saturday. Want to come?" she asked him.

"Sure, I'll ask my mum. Thanks, Monika!"

The buzzer sounded and they jumped down and ran back to class.

Just before lunch a student came in and whispered something to the teacher.

"Matthew Wade, you are wanted in the office. You may go now," said the teacher.

I don't think I've done anything wrong. Is the apartment really on fire? Has Lucky run away to come and find me?

Miss James, the school secretary, smiled at him.

"No need to look so worried, Matthew. Your mother phoned. She wanted to let you know she'll be home a bit late, and to make sure you have your key, and to tell you to let your neighbour, Mrs. Banks, know when you get home."

Matthew patted the key that he wore under his T-shirt. "Still here," he said. "Thanks, Miss James. I'll be fine. My dog will be waiting for me."

Now what did I say that for? I guess cause she's nice, and it's true. Fred is always there, waiting for me to get home, just the way Lucky used to.

But when Matthew got home, he saw Fred sitting outside the building instead of inside the apartment where he usually waited.

"Hey, Fred, you're not supposed to sit out here. Better go inside before Mister Leo sees us."

Matthew ruffled the puppy's ears, and was just about to close the front door behind them when a deep kind voice behind them asked them to wait.

"Good afternoon, my boy, glad to see you're home. Mrs. Banks wants you to come over and try her chocolate chip cookies—they're still warm from the oven!"

Matthew turned round fast. *How long had Colonel Banks been watching him and Fred?*

"Thanks very much, sir." Matthew threw his backpack in the corner and whispered, "Stay," to Fred, and locked the front door again.

Mrs. Banks put a plateful of cookies on the kitchen table, poured tea for her husband and herself and gave Matthew a glass of lemonade.

"It's so nice to have a young visitor," she said. "All our grandchildren are grown-up now and don't live close enough to visit often. Help yourself to cookies!"

"How is that dog of yours getting on, Matthew?" Colonel Banks asked him. Matthew wasn't sure which of his dogs he meant. He coughed.

"Sorry, a crumb went down the wrong way." Matthew swallowed a big gulp of lemonade. "Lucky is fine, Grandpa says, and he's turned into an excellent watchdog. It won't be much longer before my mum and I go to visit. This is Lucky." Matthew pulled out the snapshot of his dog that he kept in the back pocket of his jeans and handed it to Colonel Banks, who showed it to his wife.

"That's a handsome dog. He reminds me of the Labrador we had when our boys were young. We'd all go fishing together," Mrs. Banks said, and handed round more cookies. "Doesn't that seem a long time ago? To think we've lived in this apartment

for almost twenty-five years! It was brand new when we first moved here from Saskatoon."

Matthew put the photo back in his pocket.

"Thanks for the cookies and lemonade, Mrs. Banks. I'd better go home and get started on my homework before my mum gets home!" Matthew said, standing up.

"You are welcome any time, my dear," the old lady said.

The colonel walked across the hall with Matthew. "Don't forget to wish on the new moon tomorrow night. Do you know the routine?"

Matthew shook his head.

"Hold a new penny in your hand and bow to the moon as soon as it appears. Close your eyes before you make your wish and turn around three times." The colonel handed Matthew a shiny new penny.

"Thanks a lot, sir. And does the wish come true?" Matthew asked the colonel.

"Sometimes it does. I always think it's worth a try! Good luck."

"Did you hear that, Fred? I'm going to do exactly what he told me." He opened the door to their apartment and went inside.

Matthew's mother came home a few minutes later and asked him if he was hungry, so he told her about the cookies and how nice the colonel and Mrs. Banks had been.

"And Monika invited me to her birthday party on Saturday!" said Matthew.

Mrs. Wade looked at the address on the card. "That sounds like fun, what do you think she'd like for a present?"

"A book about keeping goldfish. Her fish die pretty fast!"

"Good idea, we'll buy it on Friday after school. I'll phone Monika's mother and tell her you'll be there. Why don't you ask her to come and play after school one day next week? We could both walk her home after supper. She doesn't live far from us."

"Okay, I'll ask her."

I'll have to make some excuse about Fred or she'll know he's not real. She's my friend, so she'll understand. Or will she say I've been telling lies?

CHAPTER NINE

Break-in

"Did you have a good time?" Mrs. Wade asked Matthew when she picked him up after Monika's birthday party on Saturday.

"It was neat, we decorated our own cupcakes. They were shaped like goldfish, but Monika wouldn't eat hers. She said, 'I'd feel like I was eating my own pets.' She can be pretty weird sometimes."

Matthew had been thinking all day about what Colonel Banks had told him about wishing on the new moon. Now he stood at the window of his room, waiting for the moon to appear.

"I'm going to make my big wish any minute, Fred," Matthew said. "You're in my head so you know what I'm thinking and what my wish is going to be. Don't feel bad, okay?" He patted Fred. "You'll always be my friend, and we'll have great times together, but Lucky was my first dog and it's not the same without him."

Matthew pointed to the sky, his penny ready in his hand. "There's the moon now, just coming out above the building across the parking lot. Here goes..."

He bowed, and turned around three times with his eyes shut, making his wish. When he opened them again, he saw someone or something moving, stooping low at the far end of the parking lot.

"Sit, Fred. Stay. Someone's out there, trying to look like a shadow. He's moving along the wall, keeping out of the moonlight. He's looking into the windows of all the cars. Keep down!" Matthew crouched beside Fred, hoping whoever it was wouldn't see him.

"He's coming closer. He's right beside Mister Leo's red truck. The guy's holding a brick in his hand. No!" The shattering of glass sounded like a peal of thunder. "He's smashed the side window.

He's putting his arm through so he can open the door. Go get him, Fred! Run, don't let him get away!" Matthew shouted with all his might, leaning out of the open window, and letting out the loudest woof he'd ever managed. "That'll scare him away!"

Lights came up in all the windows. Mister Leo rushed out, talking on his cellphone. He ran to the end of the lot and disappeared down the alley. Flashing lights appeared, police sirens screamed and tenants ran outside, some in their nightclothes.

Matthew saw Colonel Banks talking to some of their neighbours, waving his walking stick. He noticed Matthew leaning out of the window and saluted him. Matthew waved back, jumping up and down with excitement.

"I bet Mister Leo called the police. Maybe some of the tenants did too. We did that Fred—we scared the thief and warned everyone. Woof!"

"Matthew Wade! Stop that noise!" Matthew's mother came running into the room, shut the

window and pulled down the blinds. "What's got into you?"

"Mum, Fred and me scared the robber! Fred was really brave. I wish you'd seen him. Don't be mad. Come here, Fred. Good dog. You're a hero."

"I don't want to hear another word about Fred. This game has gone too far. Are you trying to get us evicted?" Mrs. Wade asked.

"But, Mum, it's not a game. This was for real..."

"I am going to tell you one last time, and I want you to listen. Fred does not exist. It's pretend. It's okay as long as you remember that it's only a game, and don't bother our neighbours. When you make this kind of a disturbance, how am I going to explain you're playing with an invisible dog?"

"Mum, you don't understand. Fred and I both saw him. There was a real live robber out there. I barked like this—woof, woof—and it scared him off."

"I don't know what to do with you, Matthew. You are deliberately not hearing me. We will talk about this in the morning. And now there's someone at the door. It'll be Mister Leo, not that I can blame him!"

Mrs. Wade left the room to speak to the manager.

"She's really mad at us, Fred," Matthew whispered. "Don't worry, I'm telling the truth, and Mister Leo knows it. Mum will have to believe us. There was a robber out there. He did smash the side window of the truck, and we saw it. It wasn't a dream, and it wasn't pretend."

CHAPTER TEN

A Witness

Matthew heard his mother open the door and ask the visitor in. It wasn't Mr. Leo.

"Good evening, Mrs. Wade. I'm Constable Mike Williams. Mister Leo, the manager, phoned 9-1-1. I won't keep you long."

"Please sit down, Constable. I'm afraid it's all been a dreadful mistake. I'm sorry you were called out. My son is responsible for the noise. I talked to him about it, and I can guarantee it won't happen again."

Matthew pulled on his jeans, walked barefoot into the living room and stood beside his mother.

"This is my son, Matthew." Mrs. Wade looked at her son reproachfully. The constable shook Matthew's hand.

"Good to meet you, Matthew. We were called in when you and your dog discovered the intruder."

"Constable, I can explain! You see, it's a game my son plays. He has a vivid imagination."

Matthew clutched the leash, hoping it would give him the courage to speak up.

"No, Mum, it wasn't a game. We saw everything from my window."

"I'd like to take a look at the window from which you observed the disturbance, Matthew, and to ask you a few questions. May I, Mrs. Wade?"

Matthew and his mother led the way into the bedroom, and she hastily straightened the quilt and pillows.

Constable Williams raised the blinds, opened the window and leaned out. Then he turned back to Matthew, taking out his notebook and pencil.

"Was the window open or closed this evening?"

"It was open," Matthew said. "My mum didn't come in to close it until after I barked."

The constable wrote in his notebook.

"Are you going to write down everything I say?"
Matthew asked.

"Yes, I am. That's my job. Please start at the beginning and tell me every detail you remember."

"I was standing right here at the window, waiting for the new moon to come out, talking to my dog, Fred…"

"Fred is your dog, right?"

"Yes, sir. He's invisible, so only I can see him. My real dog, Lucky, is the one in the photograph on the mantel. I told Fred that I was going to make a wish on the new moon and that he shouldn't be jealous. He's in my head, so he knows what I'm thinking."

The constable said, "I understand. Carry on, you're doing fine!"

"When I opened my eyes after I made my wish, I saw a shadow at the back of the parking lot. I knew it hadn't been there before. I'm pretty sure it was a guy."

"What was he wearing?" the constable asked.

"He wore dark rugby pants and a dark jacket—navy or black, I guess. The hood was pulled low

over his eyes, so I couldn't see his face. He was big and heavy looking, taller than Mum—about as tall as you. He was looking into the windows of some of the other cars before moving toward Mister Leo's truck, the red one parked under my window."

The constable went on writing, and Matthew waited a minute before going on.

"Then I saw that the guy was holding a brick. When he raised his arm, I shouted as loud as I could to Fred, 'Go get him,' and we, um, I mean, *I* barked—woof, woof—so the guy would think Fred was a real watchdog chasing him. It didn't stop him smashing the side window of the truck, but it stopped him from stealing anything. The guy ran away, and Mister Leo came out, talking on his cell. It wasn't a game. I know Fred's not a real watchdog—he's only real to me—but I've told you the truth."

Constable Williams put away his notebook, and shook hands with Matthew again.

"You've been an excellent witness, Matthew. This description is most helpful. Thanks for your co-operation, Mrs. Wade. We'll keep Mister Leo informed. I hope you get your wish, young man. You deserve it."

As soon as she had locked the front door, Mrs. Wade hugged Matthew.

"I'm sorry. I should have believed you. I'm so proud of you, Matthew," she said. "It was brave of you to tell the constable about Fred. You're a real hero."

"Don't forget the hero's dog. Fred's a hero too," Matthew said.

"I give up. Fred's a hero too," his mother said.

CHAPTER ELEVEN

A New Sign

On Monday morning Matthew was bursting to tell Monika about the robbery, but how could he without explaining that Fred was invisible?

He asked Monika to come to his home on Wednesday, to play and stay for supper.

I'll tell her then, he thought. *I'll have to!*

"Wednesday is spaghetti night," he told Monika.

"I love spaghetti. I finished that book on goldfish you gave me on Saturday. It's great! I found out some really helpful hints. Maybe I've been giving them too much food! How are Fred and Lucky? I can't wait to meet Fred," Monika said.

"Lucky is doing fine, I guess..." *I'm going to tell her right now. If she's my friend, she'll understand!* "And Fred, well...he feels the way I tell him to feel. He's only real in my head."

"I guessed that! I used to keep a baby unicorn in my closet. I fed him bread crusts and lettuce."

Matthew's mother met him after school. "I got off work a bit early. The landlord, Mr. Chow, phoned me at the office. He wants us to meet him in Mister Leo's office at four o'clock. Says he has something to discuss. Let's hurry and not keep him waiting."

"Maybe he wants to give Fred a medal!" said Matthew.

But his mum didn't even smile. She looked worried. "I think you'd better leave Fred inside the apartment when we go to meet Mr. Chow," she said.

Mister Leo and Colonel Banks were waiting in the office when Matthew and his mother came in. Mr. Chow stood up and introduced himself.

"I have asked Colonel Banks to be present because he represents the tenants and is greatly respected by all of us. Please, Colonel, read the petition I received this morning from Mister Leo."

WE, THE UNDERSIGNED TENANTS, UNANIMOUSLY AGREE TO ASK FOR A GUARD DOG TO LIVE ON THE PREMISES. LAST NIGHT WAS THE THIRD TIME IN RECENT MONTHS THAT OUR PARKING LOT HAS BEEN VANDALIZED. IF IT HAD NOT BEEN FOR THE DOG IN APARTMENT 103, FURTHER DAMAGE WOULD HAVE MOST CERTAINLY OCCURRED.

"This is true, and I offer my thanks to you and your dog, Matthew. However, there is a problem: a guard dog must be visible to all, don't you agree?" Mr. Chow said.

"I guess so, Mr. Chow. But I do own a real guard dog—he lives on a farm with my grandfather. Lucky is just the kind of dog you are looking for. A big cross-country Labrador. I miss him and he

misses me. He would make a great watchdog. That's what he does on the farm; I trained him!"

"Then, if your mother agrees, Lucky will live here as the building watchdog. He will be a working dog, so it's not that we are making an exception to the NO PETS rule. Mrs. Wade, do you think a reduction of fifty dollars in your rent, backdated to the first of this month, is fair?"

Mrs. Wade looked at Matthew, who nodded.

"Thank you, Mr. Chow," Mrs. Wade said. "That sounds more than fair. I will ask my father to bring Lucky to Vancouver in his truck this weekend."

"Colonel Banks has offered to walk Lucky around the building and parking lot every morning and afternoon while your son is at school. He tells me he is used to Labradors. At night Lucky will sleep in the parking lot under your window, Matthew. You will advise Mister Leo about a suitable kennel."

"Thank you, sir, but please, no chain. Lucky wouldn't like a chain."

Mister Leo opened his mouth to speak. He did not look pleased.

Mr. Chow silenced him with a look and said, "I understand—a farm dog is used to freedom. No chain, it's agreed. And now you will wish to go and tell your other dog, isn't that so?"

Mr. Chow shook hands with Matthew and his mother. Colonel Banks winked at Matthew.

I'll offer to do his recycling and take out the garbage for him and Mrs. Banks forever. I'll start today, after supper, Matthew decided.

The next day a sign was posted in the mailroom:

IN RESPONSE TO TENANTS' REQUEST,
THE FOLLOWING CHANGE WILL BE
EFFECTIVE AS OF OCTOBER 1:
IN THE INTEREST OF TENANT SAFETY
AND SECURITY, A GUARD DOG WILL
PERMANENTLY RESIDE ON THE PREMISES.

S. CHOW, PROPERTY OWNER
R. LEO, RESIDENT MANAGER

Fred and Matthew helped Mister Leo to put up signs on the front and back of the building that read: GUARD DOG ON PREMISES.

Back in his room, Matthew sat down to have a talk with Fred. "Don't worry Fred, you get a sign of your own too. I'm making it, see—**BEWARE OF THE DOG**. I'll prop it up against the window. And guess what, Fred? You get to sleep here with me the way you always have."

In the kitchen Mrs. Wade heard the sound of happy barking and shook her head, wondering, "How did we end up with two dogs?"

THE END

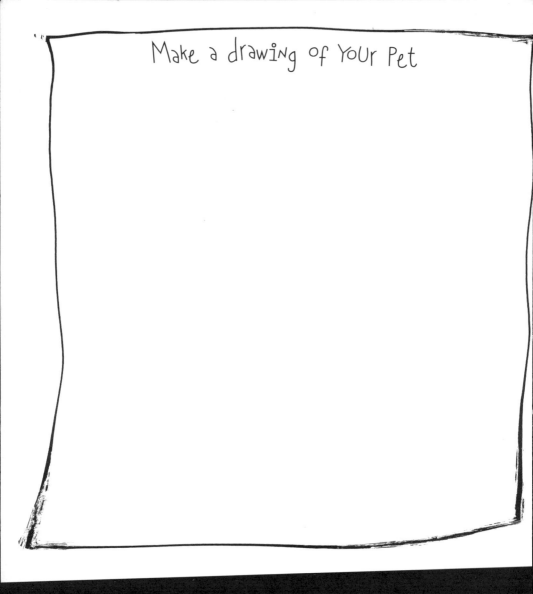

Make a drawing of your Pet

About the Author and Illustrator

Irene N. Watts has won many prizes for her writing, including the GEOFFREY BILSON AWARD FOR HISTORICAL FICTION. *A Telling Time* was given a special mention by WHITE RAVEN for its contribution to international understanding among cultures and people. *No Pets Allowed* was inspired by her son's invisible childhood friend. Irene lives in Vancouver with her family, which includes seven dogs.

Kathryn E. Shoemaker has illustrated several books for Tradewind, including *Floyd the Flamingo* and *A Telling Time*. Her book *My Animal Friends* was chosen for British Columbia's READY, SET, LEARN early literacy program.

A NOTE ABOUT THE ILLUSTRATIONS The illustrations in this book were rendered on scratchboard and in coloured black pencil on Clearprint vellum. First the imaginary dog was drawn on scratchboard and then scanned and printed at a lighter greyscale directly onto the Clearprint vellum. Next the rest of the characters and their settings were drawn onto the Clearprint vellum with black coloured pencil.